ELIZABETH WINTHROP

SQUASHED IN THE MIDDLE

ILLUSTRATED BY

PAT CUMMINGS

HENRY HOLT AND COMPANY · NEW YORK

Henry Holt and Company, LLC
Publishers since 1866
175 Fifth Avenue, New York, New York 10010
www.henryholtchildrensbooks.com

Henry Holt® is a registered trademark of Henry Holt and Company, LLC.
Text copyright © 2005 by Elizabeth Winthrop
Illustrations copyright © 2005 by Pat Cummings
All rights reserved. Distributed in Canada by H. B. Fenn and Company Ltd.

Library of Congress Cataloging-in-Publication Data
Winthrop, Elizabeth.
Squashed in the middle / by Elizabeth Winthrop;
illustrated by Pat Cummings.—1st ed.
p.   cm.
Summary: When Daisy, a middle child, is invited to spend the night
at her friend's house, her family finally pays attention to her.
ISBN-13: 978-0-8050-6497-1
ISBN-10: 0-8050-6497-4
[1. Middle-born children—Fiction. 2. Identity—Fiction. 3. Assertiveness
(Psychology)—Fiction. 4. Sleepovers—Fiction.] I. Cummings, Pat, ill. II. Title.
PZ7.W768Dai 2005   [E]—dc22   2004010135
First Edition—2005 / Designed by Donna Mark
The artist used watercolor, gouache, colored pencil, and pastel
to create the illustrations for this book.
Printed in China on acid-free paper. ∞

10 9 8 7 6 5 4 3 2

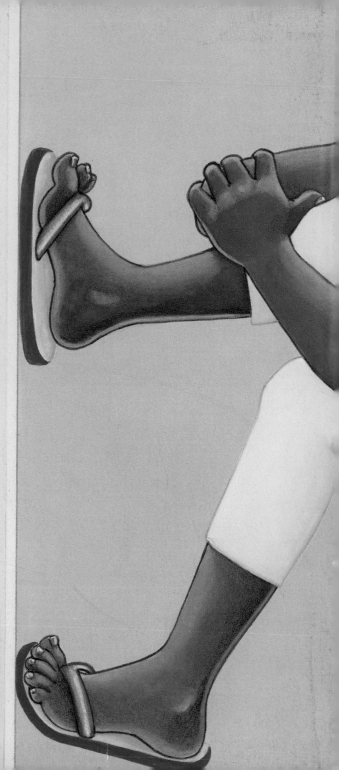

For Emily Ruth Alsop, who steals the show
even when she's in the chorus
—E. W.

For Bill Morris
—P. C.

Daisy was squashed right in the middle of her noisy family.

She had one older sister and one younger brother.

They talked to Daisy,
they talked about Daisy,
and they talked
right over Daisy's head.
But when Daisy talked,
nobody ever listened.

"Daisy's very shy,"
her mother told the butcher.

"Daisy uses the pink-and-green
toothbrush," her sister told
the baby-sitter.

"Daisy doesn't like apple pie,"
her father told the waitress.

"I'll eat hers,"
her brother said.

"I like blueberries,"
Daisy said.

But nobody
listened to her.

Rosa was Daisy's new friend.
She lived next door.

"Daisy, will you sleep over
at my house?" Rosa asked
one afternoon.

"Daisy has never slept over
at someone's house before,"
said her mother.

"I've slept at Grandma's,"
said Daisy.

But her mother
did not hear her.

"She won't go anywhere without her stuffed duck,"
said her brother.

"She'll come home in the middle of the night,"
said her sister in her big-know-it-all voice.

"No, I won't," said Daisy.

But nobody heard her.

Maybe they're right,
Daisy thought.

Daisy ran to her room and
hid in the closet.

A little later, Rosa knocked
on the door and whispered,
"Daisy, open up."

"Is anybody else there?" Daisy asked.

"No," said Rosa. "Just me."

Daisy opened the door.
"I want to spend the night
at your house," she said.

"I'll help you get ready," said Rosa.

They packed Daisy's nightgown
and her pink-and-green toothbrush
and her stuffed duck.

"I'm going to spend the night at Rosa's house," Daisy told her family.

But nobody heard her.

Her father was
chopping carrots.

Her sister was chasing her brother
around and around the kitchen table.

Her mother was talking on the phone.

So Daisy and Rosa left.

But nobody noticed.

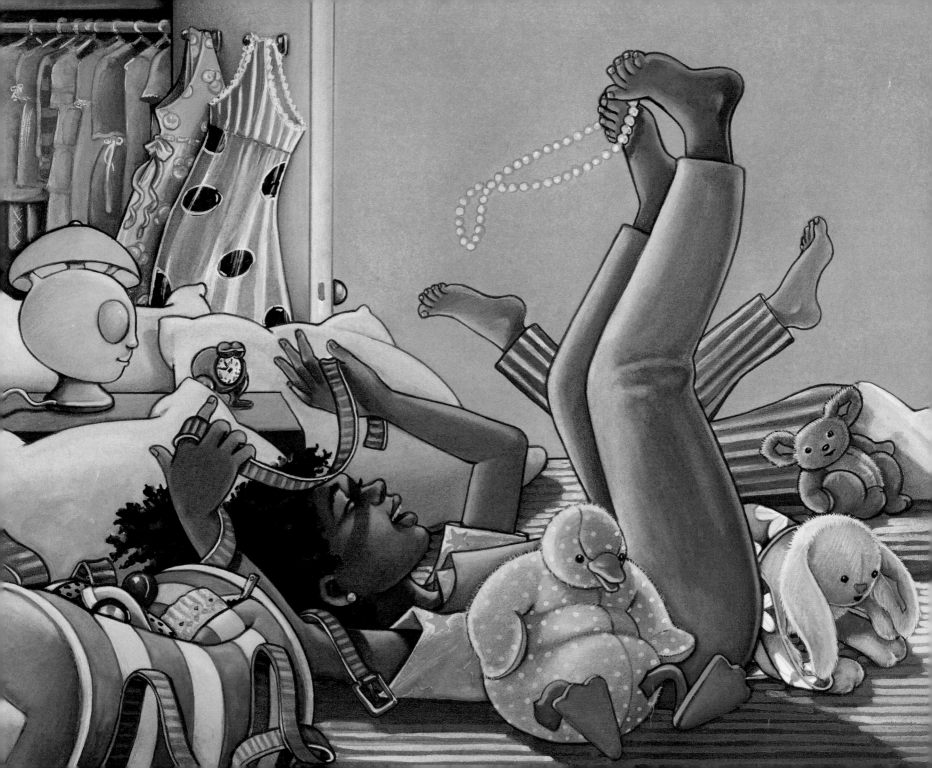

Daisy put her stuffed duck on the extra bed
in Rosa's room and hung her nightgown in the closet.
She stuck her pink-and-green toothbrush in the glass
next to Rosa's blue one.

"There," said Daisy. "Now I'm here."

"Let's have a snack," said Rosa.

Suddenly there was a knock at the door.
Rosa stood on a chair and peeked
through the peek hole.

"They're here," she said.

She opened the door.

There stood Daisy's whole family.

"We looked everywhere for you,"
said Daisy's father.

"I already told you," said Daisy,
"I'm spending the night at Rosa's house."

"You did?" said Daisy's mother.

"We came to take you home,"
said Daisy's sister in her
big-know-it-all voice.

"I'M NOT GOING

"I'm spending the night here."

"But you'll get homesick," said Daisy's sister.

"NO, I WON'T," said Daisy.

"Stop shouting," said her brother.

"I HAVE TO SHOUT," said Daisy.

"Why?" her mother asked.

"Because I tell you things, but nobody ever listens to me."

The whole family stared at Daisy.

HOME!" shouted Daisy.

"I think it's time for us to go home,"
said Daisy's father.
He gave Daisy a good-night hug.

"Have fun," said Daisy's mother.
She gave Daisy a good-night kiss.

"Don't forget to brush your teeth,"
said her sister in her
big-know-it-all voice.

"Can I have her ice cream?"
her brother asked.

"Good-bye, good night, sleep tight,"
Daisy said.
And she shut the door with a bang.

"Now we can have a snack," said Rosa.

Daisy and Rosa ate blueberries
and played with their stuffed animals
and brushed their teeth
and stayed up late.

In the morning when Daisy got home,
she told her family all about her sleepover.

And, for the first time, everybody listened.